Katie
and the
Lemon Tree

Books by Esther Bender

Lemon Tree Series
Katie and the Lemon Tree
Virginia and the Tiny One

Picture Storybooks
April Bluebird
The Crooked Tree
Search for a Fawn

Mystery
Shadow at Sun Lake

Meditations
A Cry from the Clay

Study Guide for *Katie and the Lemon Tree*
In Treasure Hunt Series,
John Hopkins University Teacher-Training Program

Study Guides for *The Crooked Tree* and *Search for a Fawn*
From B & B Books, c/o Esther Bender,
25 Sunset Drive, Cumberland, MD 21502-1927

Katie
and the
Lemon Tree

Esther Bender

Illustrated by Joy Dunn Keenan

HERALD PRESS
Scottdale, Pennsylvania
Waterloo, Ontario

Library of Congress Cataloging-in-Publication Data
Bender, Esther, 1942-
    Katie and the lemon tree/Esther Bender : illustrated
by Joy Dunn Keenan.
      p.   cm.
    Summary: Chronicles the life of Katie and her hus-
band Daniel who emigrate from Germany to the United
States to build a life for themselves and their family,
while struggling to keep the religious faith so important
in Katie's upbringing.
    ISBN 0-8361-3657-8 (permanent paper)
    [1. Emigration and immigration–Fiction. 2. Frontier
and pioneer life–Fiction. 3. German Americans–Fiction.
4. Christian life–Fiction. 5. Family life–Fiction.]
I. Keenan, Joy Dunn, 1952-   ill. II. Title.
PZ7.B43137Kat   1994
[Fic]–dc20   94-2581

The paper used in this publication is recycled and meets
the minimum requirements of American National Standard for Information Sciences—Permanence of Paper for
Printed Library Materials, ANSI Z39.48-1984.

Scripture is adapted from *The Holy Bible, King James
Version.*

KATIE AND THE LEMON TREE
Copyright © 1994 by Herald Press, Scottdale, Pa. 15683
    Published simultaneously in Canada by Herald Press,
    Waterloo, Ont. N2L 6H7. All rights reserved
Library of Congress Catalog Number: 94-2581
International Standard Book Number: 0-8361-3657-8
Printed in the United States of America
Book design Jim Butti

03 02 01 00 10 9 8 7 6 5 4 3

10,500 copies in print

To order or request information, please call
1-800-759-4447 (individuals); 1-800-245-7894 (trade).
Website: www.mph.org

**To my mother,
for hours and hours of reading**

Contents

The Promise! The Dream! 9

1. Farewell to Friends 13
2. Farewell to Family 19
3. Journey by Faith 24
4. Can This Be America? 26
5. Journey's End 31
6. Settling In 34
7. Planting the Seed 36
8. Seed Money 41
9. Sweet Harvest 45
10. The Stone Pile 48
11. The Price of a Tree 52
12. Longings 55
13. Passing Years 59
14. Remembering 64
15. Risking It All 68
16. Pruning 71
17. Swellings 75
18. Bees' Work 77
19. Evening 80
20. A New Generation 84

Notes 90
Bible References 92
The Author 93

The Promise!
The Dream!

We all remember the Pilgrims who came to America for religious freedom in the 1600s. Then in the 1700s and 1800s—from England, the Netherlands, Italy, Germany, France, and other countries—men, women, and children streamed across the ocean to North America.

William Penn and Lord Baltimore had invited them to settle the states of Pennsylvania and Maryland. There were Quakers, Lutherans, Methodists, Presbyterians, Catholics, Amish, Mennonites, and others, drawn by the promise of religious freedom and free land.

All were immigrants. All became Americans. In North America, everybody's family was once an immigrant family. Even the ancestors of Native Americans came from somewhere else.

From what country did your family come? When? Years ago some people in your family tree came to America. They left home forever, or you would not be here. Who were they—grandfather, great-great grandmother, a long-ago ancestor? Were they Irish, English, African, German, Swiss? Or several of these?

Ask your parents and grandparents these questions. You might find answers in genealogy books. People who write such books search old records, like detectives, and write down many bits of information, dates and names and places.

There is yet a deeper puzzle. *Why* did your people come to America? Were they tired of the religious wars of old Europe? Were they poor, needing a fresh start? Were they brought here as slaves and servants?

Many came for free land and religious freedom. *Religious freedom!* Empty words from a history book! What do they mean to young Katie Miller, as she bids farewell to her homeland forever, crosses the Atlantic Ocean with her young husband, Daniel, and finds their own homestead? Why could she stand to be seasick on the way and homesick after arriving?

When her mama kissed Katie good-bye and said, "Katie, keep the faith!" what did she mean?

Katie is true-to-life fiction. Listen to the "Good-bye Song," really sung years ago. Listen as the wind flaps the sails. Smell the rotting fish of Baltimore harbor. Hear that "lemons won't grow here." Jolt with the Miller couple on the wagon, searching for a farm in a cool mountain valley, near new friends. Dream with Katie as she tries to grow that lemon tree.

Katie came for a promise of freedom.

She found room for a dream....

1

Farewell to Friends

Listen! They are singing in the village.
Listen! They are weeping in the village.
From time long past,
from a place long forgotten
comes the echo of their songs,
the songs of faith.

Katie Miller clung to Daniel's hand. Around them, singing, the youths of the German village circled with hands joined.

Among them was Katie's sister, Maria—Maria with gray-green eyes like her own. Katie's eyes filled with tears. She, Katie, was leaving, going to America.

Maria is only fifteen. I may never see her again, thought Katie.

She glanced at Daniel. His thick, dark eyebrows pulled together, making furrows in his forehead. His lips were drawn into thin creases.

He looked as he had when they buried his mother, six years ago. Katie well remembered that day. At fourteen, she liked the strength in his face as he struggled with his feelings.

Now, Daniel brushed his dark, wavy hair back with his free hand. He smiled at her. She looked away, not wanting him to see her sorrow.

Daniel doesn't want me to know how hard leaving is for him. He's strong for me.

His hand was as moist as on their wedding day, a year ago, when she had no thoughts of leaving Germany. He had talked about land of their own, but she passed it off lightly. Others had gone to America, yes, but they were adventurous, not of Daniel's hardworking kinfolk or of Katie's serious family.

She didn't blame Daniel. If anyone was responsible, Daniel's father was. Before his death, he told Daniel, "Take the little money I leave you and go to America."

Katie understood his father's wish. Owning land was an impossible dream in Germany. Farms were owned by stately families and handed down from father to son. The villagers, Katie among them, knew they would spend a lifetime working the fields for those of high birth.

Yes, she understood. No, she didn't blame Daniel. But she was surprised when his father's wish grew into her husband's desire, then into full-blown plans.

"Daniel has always been a dreamer," her mother commented.

"We *can* have land," Daniel declared. "In America, we *can* have land." His jaw was set.

Then he smiled. "For you, Katie, and for our children, I want land."

He wants so much for us—our own land in America. Our own farm!

She squeezed his damp hand. His fingers tightened around hers.

We are leaving Germany forever. Daniel says we will come back if America is not what we want. But we won't come back. I know we never will. I want Papa and Mama and Maria and David to join us someday.

She glanced around the circle of friends who had come to bid farewell. Soon they would sing the "Good-bye Song," just as she had sung it for others. Many from surrounding villages had gone to America.

A year ago, the weaver left their village, and they had sung the song for him. He went to America because he didn't want to serve in the king's army. Like the families of Katie and Daniel, the weaver set out to follow the way of Jesus, to love and forgive, not to fight and kill.

In the end, Katie agreed to go to America for the sake of their children. Daniel said their children, born in America, would never know the fear they felt in Germany.

Katie had always known fear. She had heard stories of earlier centuries, how the blood of faithful martyrs flowed freely. Even now, those of her faith were often slighted by others. Katie and Daniel worshiped with the quiet ones.

Now Katie wanted peace for her unborn children. For them, she agreed to cross the great Atlantic Ocean, a sea over which few returned.

Our children—who will they marry in America? Will they have dark hair and eyes like Daniel's, or green eyes and lighter hair like mine? What kind of home will we have?

She remembered the packets of dried flower seeds, taken from her mother's garden and packed carefully among her clothes.

I will make us a home. Wherever we live, I will plant flowers.

Katie's sister, Maria, glowed with a special smile as she moved by. Katie smiled in return, then shut her eyes.

She willed herself to remember the sounds of Germany: cattle bawling; her friends, one voice after another singing and fading behind her; the shuf, shuf, shuf of the shoes, scuffing on the ground to the rhythm of the song.

The "Good-bye Song" began. Fighting back tears, Katie opened her eyes and sang along.

Nun ist die Zeit und Stunde da,
 dass wir fahren nach Amerika.

Now have come the time and hour
 To travel to America.

The "Good-bye Song" began as Katie fought back tears.

When the song ended, Katie fled into her parent's cottage. Upstairs, the moonlight beckoned her to the window. She wept as she watched her friends go home. Her mother came and stood by her in silence. Then Daniel came upstairs, and her mother padded softly downstairs.

They undressed in silence. Daniel, first in bed, lifted Mama's coverlet to welcome her. He cradled her head against the silky, warm skin of his inner arm and covered her. He held her close and sighed.

"We'll have a good life, I promise you," he whispered.

Katie didn't answer. Tonight was for grieving. Tomorrow, they would leave.

2

Farewell to Family

Listen! Listen! Mama's singing.

Next morning, Katie was awakened by the sound of Mama singing downstairs. The song quivered and died. Katie heard a cough and a half-sob, then the clank of metal that meant Mama was feeding the fire. "Flup, flup, flup," her wooden spoon beat batter in the bowl.

Without opening her eyes, Katie reached for Daniel. The bedding was cool and empty. He was already gone. She swung her feet onto the cold floor, crossed the room, and opened the shutters. Outside, the sun made steam of last night's dew. A white haze hung over the rich green fields. She dressed and hurried down to breakfast.

Papa, sitting at the table, cleared his throat. "Sit down, Katie! Eat well!"

She obeyed without thought. Her eyes were on Daniel, who smiled at her from the bench behind the table. "I let you sleep. The trip will be hard."

Mama padded back and forth from kettle to table. She filled Katie's bowl with thick gruel and handed her a pitcher of sweet milk and a slice of crusty bread. Katie began to eat.

Maria came to the table. Her thick, rust-blond hair was braided and coiled around her head. Maria reached up and touched her braids. "Here, take this," she offered, handing Katie the ivory comb, the one hair ornament they owned. Lovely in its simplicity, Maria and Katie had often fought over it.

"Maria, I can't."

"You must, Katie. I would never be happy wearing it again with you gone so far away. Take it, please."

Seeing her sister's earnest face, Katie tucked the precious comb into a pocket hidden in the folds of her clothing.

"They're coming!" shouted their brother David as he dashed in from the morning milking. Through the open door came the clop of hooves and the jingle of harness. Wagon wheels ground on the courtyard stones.

Daniel shoved back from the table, nearly upsetting the bench in his rush to join his two older brothers outside. They had come, with their families, in two wagons. One brother would take both their families home after the last good-byes. The other would take Katie and Daniel on the first leg of their journey to America.

Katie swallowed one more bite of bread and

washed it down with milk. She tried to lock into her memory the taste of Mama's bread, the dishes on the table, the tendrils of gray hair on either side of Mama's face, and Papa's nostrils, pinched white from hiding his inner pain.

"Wait!" cried Papa. "The blessing." They bowed their heads. Katie's heart was too full to pray. She knew her father was praying for her and for Daniel.

"Amen." The silent prayer ended. Katie stood up and wrapped herself in Mama's best shawl, her parting gift. She followed Daniel outside. Her family filed out after her.

"Good-bye, Dan and Katie!" The family said it first, and the call was taken up by villagers who came from their houses to see them off.

Someone began the "Good-bye Song." Mama's voice, behind Katie, was a thin thread of sound that wavered in the air like a broken spiderweb.

Der wagen steht schon vor der Tür.

Now stands the wagon by the door.
    Good-bye! Good-bye!

The horses stomped, eager to be off. Again, Katie tried to hold in her memory the scent of springtime flowers, the smoke of last night's fires, the whiff of rotting dung by the cattle shed.

Good-bye to Germany forever!

Her eyes blurred with tears. She groped for her sister, Maria, and for her brother David. She hugged each in turn, then turned to her mother.

Katie's mother held her tightly and whispered, "Katie, keep the faith!"

"Yes, Mama, I will," she said.

My mother always says that. She has said it all my life. What does it mean?

"When will you come to America, Mama?"

"Someday, when it is time, when there is money."

Her father shook Daniel's hand. "Take care of our Katie," his voice boomed out. "God go with you!"

Dear Papa! Dear Daniel! Papa made Daniel promise to care for me. No one asks me to take care of Daniel, but I will. I will work hard and take care of Daniel.

The men lugged chests from the house. The larger, rough-made one settled down on the wagon with a dull thud. It held tools and seeds they would need.

They set down the second one gently, a fine old chest made by Katie's great-grandfather. It guarded their clothes and linens, the Bible, a lamp, and all their personal belongings.

"Up, Katie!" Papa gave her his hand and steadied her as she climbed into the wagon. Then Daniel was beside her.

Good-bye to Germany! Good-bye to family and friends. Auf wiedersehen! Till we meet again!

Arms stretched upward as though to pull Dan and Katie back. Singing began.

Und wenn wir sind in Baltimor,
dann heben wir die Händ' empor
und rufen laut Viktoria,
"Jetzt sind wir in Amerika."

And when we come to Baltimore,
We'll hold our hands upraised
And shout a word of victory,
"Now we're in America."

Daniel's brother clucked to the horses. The wagon wheels ground and clattered on the stones. Katie turned around and waved until her family and friends were out of sight. She wiped her tears and looked ahead. The wagon wheels seemed to sing Mama's words, *Katie, keep the faith! Katie, keep the faith!*

As they left familiar landmarks behind, Katie thought, *This is what Abraham did, in Bible times. He left his country and journeyed into a far land without knowing where he was going. God went with Abraham, and God will go with us.*

I will keep the faith, just as Mama says.

3

Journey by Faith

Good-bye to the Old World! Hello to the New World!

On the ship to America, the immigrants needed to get ready to use the common language of their new home.

Twice each day, midmorning and midafternoon, Katie, Daniel, and others interested in learning English gathered in the ship's dining room. By the captain's arrangement, a teacher helped them start to speak English.

During rough weather, Katie and Daniel stilled their fears by practicing new words. Later they clung to a rail on the deck of the ship.

Only a few passengers had come on deck so soon after the storm. A month into the voyage, this was the best place to escape the smell of seasickness in the hold. Here they could breathe fresh air and be alone.

Katie watched the skyline slide up and down as the ship sank into a trough, then rose on the crest of each wave. Wind snapped the sails. Beneath them, the water rumbled.

The summer storm was over, and she was glad, *so* glad to see blue sky again.

"America—how will it look?" She often asked that question. Talking about America kept her spirits up and helped her bear the seasickness.

"Trees everywhere, they tell me," Daniel said. "We will clear land for crops, and we will build—a barn—a house. Life will be hard. We will work and work, but in the end, it will be ours."

Katie closed her eyes and saw a house, a yard, and flowers grown from the seeds Mama had given her. They would make a home, just as in Germany. She would have the same flowers Mama had, but there would be something more. Katie was sure of it, something she could not yet imagine. She was content in knowing just that.

The ship creaked. The air smelled of rope and saltwater. Voices of passengers were drifting up from below. Water, endless water surrounded them. With each snap, the sails sang to her, *Katie, keep the faith! Katie, keep the faith!*

That night, before she fell asleep, a voice seemed to sing in her head, *God is watching, rocking, singing you to sleep, Katie!*

She smiled. Mama was praying for her, asking God to do the rocking. They would reach America safely.

Katie slept.

4

Can This Be America?

Seagulls wheeled over the ship. They came from where the ship was headed and disappeared in the same direction. Plump and feisty, they squawked for crumbs of food.

Land must be near, thought Katie. *Soon we will reach America.*

Daniel's fingers tapped the rails. His head was thrown back. A breeze blew his dark hair off his forehead as he scanned the horizon.

Soon, soon we'll reach America.

In August they arrived at Baltimore, and the big ship edged into the harbor. The stench of rotting fish was in the air. The weather was sweltering.

Katie tasted the saltiness of the sweat that ran down her face. *Can this be America? Have we made a dreadful mistake and sailed somewhere else?*

"Katie! We're here!" exclaimed Daniel, laughing. He picked her up and swung her around on the deck until she was dizzy.

She was gasping for breath. "Are you sure this is Baltimore?"

"Balt-i-mo ha-bo (harbor)," chanted a black man on the dock. He secured the gangplank.

Passengers pushed off, propelling Daniel and Katie in front of them. Katie waited on the dock while Daniel returned for their chests.

What a strange place! Katie was filled with wonder. Wooden docks and sheds; dirt and noise; white people rushing, yelling; black people, backs bare and sweating; black people pulling, pushing, loading and unloading boxes, barrels, and bags. *Where are the trees?*

Katie stood by their belongings to guard them while Daniel went to buy a horse and wagon. Restlessly, she shaded her eyes from the glaring sun and took a step backward, colliding with someone behind her. Crash! Yellow fruits rolled. A dockhand scurried to pick them up.

"*Es tut mir leid.* I'm sorry!" Katie dropped to her knees to help gather the fruits. "What are these?" She felt the rubbery skin.

"Lemons! Have one," the man offered. "Alone, it's sour, but if you put the juice in water with sugar, it makes a drink fit for kings. It came on that ship from the South." He pointed.

"*Danke! Thanks!*" Katie gave him a shy smile

as she grasped the lemon.

"Won't grow here," the dockhand added. "Too cold, ma'am." He swung the wooden crate on one shoulder and swaggered off, singing loudly.

Katie poked the lemon with a finger. A bit of juice oozed onto her hand. She licked it. Too sour!

What should she do with the lemon? Thoughtfully, she opened the trunk and placed it inside the cook pot. She would save it for a while. Maybe she would try that American drink. She could think of no reason to keep it, but, in this new place, it was best to learn about everything.

She shut the trunk and turned toward a rumbling sound. Daniel was coming with their new wagon. He halted beside her.

I'm so proud of my Daniel! He's whistling! He's full of hope for our new life, she thought.

She helped Daniel load their possessions in the wagon. He gave her a hand up to the seat. They were on their way to the West, where land was cheap.

The ship had rocked her. Now the rough streets of Baltimore made her teeth chatter. Then she remembered.

"The song, Daniel!" she exclaimed. "Let's sing the song."

"What song?"

"You know. *'Und wenn wir sind in Baltimor.'* "

Daniel's voice joined hers.

The dockhand swaggered off while Katie poked the lemon with a finger.

And when we come to Baltimore,
    We'll hold our hands upraised
And shout a word of victory.

He lifted his arms, reins in his hands.

Katie lifted her arms, too. Together they shouted, *"Jetzt sind wir in Amerika.* Now we're in America."

They turned down a cobblestone street. As the cobbles shook the wagon, Katie felt her cheeks shake. Between jolts, she said, "I . . . did not think . . . America would . . . look like . . . this!"

5

Journey's End

They had been traveling west for weeks, by day riding the wagon's rough wooden seat or walking, at night sleeping in the wagon near farm buildings.

Katie was so tired her bones ached. The ruts of many wagon wheels jerked them from side to side. Katie swayed with the wagon. Between bumps, her eyes closed and her head fell sideways. She was *so* drowsy.

She wondered where they would spend the night. They hadn't passed a single homestead since morning.

Another hill ahead! Each mountain was higher than the last. Katie no longer wondered if there were trees in America. Trees stood on each side of the narrow road and joined branches overhead.

A frost had painted the edges of the leaves in

autumn's first touches of red. Sometimes broken branches were in the road. Daniel removed them when he could so the road would be clear for the next travelers.

The sun was low in the sky as they approached a clearing.

"Whoa!" called Daniel. "Here we rest."

The horse stopped. As Katie jumped down, she heard a shout from the forest. Toward them strode a tall man, dressed in brown. A small plump woman followed, then two girls and a boy.

"*Willkommen!* Welcome!" The man extended his hand. "My wife, Sarah, and the children, Mark, Elizabeth, Mary! Paul Hostetler's the name."

"Daniel Miller," responded Daniel, "and my wife, Katie—*aus Deutschland*, from Germany. We're looking for land to homestead, or to buy if the price is small."

Sarah threw up her arms in delight. "You're from Germany, the homeland! Come! You will stay the night with us and tell us the news."

Katie followed Sarah to the cabin. The small woman bustled about, cooking an abundant meal. All the while, she plied Katie with questions about Germany and Baltimore.

Over dinner that night, Paul said there was cheap land for settling nearby. Daniel's eyes questioned Katie's. She nodded assent. When Sarah said there was a village five miles away, with a store and smithy, Katie's eyes lit up.

The lonely road they traveled had led Katie to

think they had passed the last town many miles back. Paul explained that most settlers nearby had come south from the plateaus of Pennsylvania, then east. He said land was settled west of them, also.

The high hardwood and pine forests where the Hostetlers lived was the most remote land and the last to be claimed. If the Millers were willing to settle in these mountains, they could buy land by cutting a share of its timber for the owner. Only a token sum of money would be needed.

The Hostetlers offered silent prayers at the end of the meal. Katie felt they were among family. By the time they left the table, she wanted to settle near these warm and happy friends. She was delighted to find that Daniel felt the same.

Late in the night, talk ceased. Katie and Daniel slept on the floor beside the fireplace. Next morning, Katie helped Sarah with the milking while Paul took Daniel to find out about the land.

When they returned, Daniel declared, "It's done! We have sixty-six acres of land!"

6

Settling In

Paul and Sarah insisted that Dan and Katie stay with them until a cabin was built. As Katie snuggled under a blanket before the fire each night, she thought how happy they were to find such kind friends.

One night words popped into her mind: *God has kept faith with us.* The thought surprised her. Could it be that faith was give and take? No. How silly! Mama would know the answer to that. She must write and ask her.

Dan chopped and sawed trees into logs. Paul helped when he could spare the time. They cut and notched the logs to build a cabin. It was urgent to have shelter before winter. Later Daniel would harvest logs to pay for the land.

Katie, and sometimes Sarah, gathered small stones for chinking. They mixed clay with horsehair, straw, and feathers to make mud paste, daub for the walls. Patiently they pressed the stones between the logs of the new cabin and applied the mud. Finally, a last coat of mud was smoothed over the joints and left to dry.

Daniel cut rocks for the fireplace. Paul helped him heave the stones in place. When Indian summer arrived, the one-room cabin was done.

The one-room cabin had a fireplace for cooking and heating.

7

Planting the Seed

"This is ours, all ours."

Katie said the words aloud as she stood in the doorway. Orange and gold maple leaves whispered as they fell. A pair of gray squirrels scampered about, plumping and waving their tails.

So beautiful! thought Katie. *My new country is so beautiful!*

The chests were waiting to be unpacked. She leaned against the door and listened to the steady beat of Daniel's ax, echoing in the forest. He had said he would make a table for them today. She lingered a moment longer, then turned to her unpacking.

This chest contained their household goods. They had brought it from Paul's cabin only this morning. She brushed a dusting of green mold off the lid. Slowly, she opened it.

On top was the coverlet made by her mother.

She was struck with sudden sadness and longing to be home. Putting her face into the coverlet, her tears flowed freely. Dark blotches appeared on the fabric.

"*Jetzt sind wir in Amerika.* Now we're in America." She rocked back and forth, eyes closed, and sang the words in a soft, trembling voice.

When she stopped singing, a fresh feeling seized her. Mama was remembering her, she was sure. Mama was praying, "May my precious Katie keep the faith."

Her sadness departed and joy flowed through her body. Yes, God would keep faith with Mama. The tiny cabin seemed to glow. She stood up and hesitated. Then she danced round and round the cabin, singing and humming to herself, filled with a joy she could not explain.

At last, Katie settled down to unpack the chest. She took out plates and cups and placed them on the shelf Daniel had made. She picked up the Bible Papa had given them and placed it beside the dishes.

Katie took out the cook pot. Something inside the pot rolled back and forth.

She removed the lid and looked inside. The lemon! The poor, rotten lemon! She cut it, plucked the seeds from it, and threw the halves out the door. They disappeared among the golden leaves.

With the lemon gone, she looked at the seeds. Bits of wet flesh clung to them.

What shall I do with the lemon seeds? Katie thought.

The seeds! What shall I do with them? Plant them? How does a lemon tree look? The man said lemons will not grow here because it is too cold. But in our cabin . . . is it possible? All things are possible. Have faith like a mustard seed.

Now, she told herself, *have faith as a mustard seed.* Katie couldn't stop the thoughts or the echo of Mama's words: *Katie, keep the faith! Keep the faith!*

She took a cup from the shelf and carried it outdoors into the golden forest. She pushed back fallen leaves and filled the cup with rich black earth. Carrying the cup inside, she pressed a ring of seeds into the soil.

As she unpacked the rest of the chest, she stopped from time to time to look at the cup.

Who has seen God? her mother's voice seemed to say. She went to the door and leaned against the cabin, lost in thought, her eyes on the blue sky. She turned to the cup of soil.

Lemon seeds! I can't see them, but I know they are there! I put them there! If I plant, if I water. . . . is that faith, the planting and the watering?

The chest was empty. She pushed it in front of their one tiny window, a pane given them by Paul and Sarah. Carefully, she placed the cup with its seeds on the chest where they would have precious light.

And God will give the increase.

Strange how bits of Scripture came to her, not

in complete verses, or even in rounded thoughts, but in phrases, spoken in her Mama's voice. Many things called them forth from the depths of her mind.

Mama had sown seeds of quoted Scripture, and now, no matter what, they just grew inside Katie. All that happened to her was shaped by the Bible.

Does God honor faith about little things, like the growing of a lemon tree? Katie wondered.

8

Seed Money

Day after day, the west wind blew. It pushed snow through the crack below the door and piled up a small white drift on the floor. The cold wind frosted the window in lacy patterns.

Katie blew on the frost, melting a circle in the ice. Looking through, she saw nothing but blowing snow. Would Daniel find his way home from Hostetler's farm? She worried that some evening he might lose his way and freeze to death.

She thought of the dog the Hostetlers had given them and was glad Daniel had taken the pet along. Daniel tended cattle every day at the Hostetler's barn in exchange for hay and shelter for their horse.

Katie returned to her sewing. By the time she stitched another seam in a shirt for Daniel, the cold completely frosted the glass again. Dusk fell, and the room grew dark. She lit the lamp on the table and placed another log on the fire. It was time to put the tiny lemon tree to bed.

Only one lemon seed had sprouted. Katie kept it near the window, but it needed protection at night. Each evening, she opened the chest by the fire. From the side of the fireplace, she took a warm stone and wrapped it in a cloth. She placed the bundle in the chest. Then she set the seedling tree inside, too.

On the coldest nights, she closed the lid to hold the heat. There the tree safely waited out the night even though the fire died down to a few glowing coals while they slept.

Putting the tree into the chest was a nightly habit; she never hurried. Before shutting the lid, she often let her mind go across the ocean, home to Germany. Today, she heard her mother say, *If faith is as a seed. . . . A sprouting seed!*

If faith is as a—a lemon seed. . . . God grows the seed, but I must feed and water it.

Katie stirred the pot of stew over the fire and listened for her husband to return.

She knew Daniel was nearing the cabin door before the latch lifted because she heard a whine and scratch at the door. The dog would be sitting in the snow with one paw stroking the door. Daniel would be right behind.

There! His heavy boots packed the snow and made it screech. Being shut up alone so long had sharpened her ear for the slightest sounds.

The latch rattled. The door opened. In rushed the beagle, shaking off clouds of snow. The wind roared into all the corners, sifting white powder everywhere. Then Daniel entered, rubbing clumps of ice from his eyebrows and beard. He slammed the door shut. The sifting of white slowly melted away.

Daniel peeled off layers of clothing. Katie spread them by the fire to dry. He put on dry clothes, then lifted the lid from the stew and sniffed. "Mmmm!" The dog sat, watchful, alert.

Katie ladled out a bowlful for Daniel, another for the dog, and one for herself. They ate at the log table Daniel had made. On the floor, the dog lapped noisily.

At last, Daniel leaned back. "Paul thinks the weather will break soon. We must get sap buckets so we'll be ready for the sugaring. Paul says these maple trees make the best sugar in the world, and a good profit, too. On the first nice day, I'll go to the cooper's in the village."

Supper over, Daniel dozed by the fire. Katie got pen and ink from the log shelf. She placed them on the table by the lamp. On a precious scrap of paper, she continued her letter.

As always, she said each sentence to herself many times before she wrote. She would not waste a word. Tonight, she had one sentence for Mama, "I will pray and keep the faith until I see you coming over the hill."

She sighed. There was more she wanted to say —about the lemon tree. This long winter alone had done strange things to her. The lemon tree had become more than a tree for her. It was a seedling, but it also stood for something else.

That lemon tree was a symbol, a sign of faith. *If faith is like a mustard seed....* She had no mustard seed. *If faith be as a lemon seed....* She would keep it to herself for a while longer— no need to tell Mama yet.

Katie put away pen and ink and paper. Next she pulled down a tin box from over the fireplace. She shook it once and let it rattle, then replaced it without opening it. It held a single coin, a seed to grow money for her family to come to America. Katie and Daniel had placed it there.

But how is it to grow? How do we feed and water a coin?

The tin box over the fireplace held a single coin.

44

9

Sweet Harvest

"We will soon have church in our house—come spring," Sarah told Katie. "Four families worshiped here last year. You and Dan will make five."

Katie looked forward to that first worship service. It was not to be as soon as Sarah thought, however. The weather was a sugarmaker's dream: warm days and bitter cold nights. Sap ran freely. To boil down sap, they had to tend the fire day and night.

Spring had come with a short first thaw. Daniel and Paul tapped the maple trees in the nearby woods, making small holes through the bark with a hand drill. They pushed hollow wooden spiles into the holes and hung wooden buckets below to catch the dripping sap.

When the buckets were full, they emptied them into barrels, and rehung the empty buckets. Horses hauled the full barrels on a sled. Between sap gatherings, the men cut firewood for the boiling.

Sarah came to show Katie how to boil down the sap to syrup or sugar in a huge kettle over an outdoor fire. Katie quickly learned how to feed the fire and skim off the scum that rose to the surface of the sap. When a bubbling mass of syrup was poured into a large pan to cool, she refilled the kettle.

Soon Sarah went home to tend her own fire. Alone, Katie boiled down sap, tending the fire far into the night. Sometimes she was tempted to overload the fire or let it go untended. But each time she remembered that they had used all the coins from the tin to buy sugaring supplies. To replace the money, she would make only the finest syrup.

By the end of the season, Katie dreamed of boiling sap when she rested. On duty at the kettle, she looked toward the forest and daydreamed. Always she saw hundreds of trees bearing buckets and heard the plop, plop, plop of sap dripping into them.

By the time the run of sap slowed, they had a big supply of syrup and sugar. Daniel sold their product to the storekeeper in the village. When he returned, he gave Katie more than enough coins to replace the few he had used from the tin.

"Oh, Daniel, thank you!" Katie nearly burst with happiness.

Daniel's face, already suntanned, crinkled in

lines of a smile. His dark hair, carefully combed in Germany, now curled in ringlets around his face. Katie thought he looked handsome!

"Katie, your eyes are shining!" exclaimed Daniel as she placed the tin back on the log over the fireplace.

"Oh, Daniel, I was so afraid. . . ."

"Of what, Katie?"

"To use the money. I was afraid we would never put it back."

"You have to use it to get more, Katie. You have to invest it. That's a biblical principle."

"A biblical principle!" Katie was amazed. "But we might have lost it!"

"That's exactly what happened to the man who saved it. He lost it!

"Tomorrow, Katie, will you help pick stones? Every bit of clearing is important now. When it is time for seeding, we can only plant the land that is ready."

Her thoughts turned to planting and stone-picking. Later, when she was alone, she puzzled over saving and losing.

10

The Stone Pile

The sugaring season lasted so long it ran right into plowing time. They worked up the cleared land, then picked stones off the fields and rolled them onto a stoneboat, a flat sledge. The horses dragged them to the side of the field, where Katie and Daniel stacked them into a stone fence.

By noon that first day, Katie knew they would never finish getting all the stones off the land for this growing season.

"We bought a stone pile, Daniel!"

"Don't compare this soil to Germany's, Katie. German soil has been cultivated for hundreds of years. We will improve the land each year, and someday this soil will be rich and soft and fertile, too."

By the second day of picking stones, Katie moved in rhythm: bend, pick up, straighten, carry—bend, pick up, straighten, carry. Katie's back

They picked stones off the fields, and the horses dragged them away on a stoneboat.

ached, her head ached, her arms ached, she ached all over.

The next days blurred into each other as they worked from sunup to sundown to prepare the land in time for planting. When at last the crops were in, there was more to do: buy some chickens, fence them in, feed them, gather eggs from the hens, build the barn. Day by day, their homestead grew.

In spite of the work, Katie did not forget the lemon tree. She took it from the cup and planted it in a pot. Patiently she washed its shiny leaves and watered it.

Daniel teased her, "Katie, lemon trees won't grow here."

Katie's temper flashed. "Just wait and see!" She saw lemons in her mind, lemons on her tree.

Daniel shook his head. "You spend all that time washing that little tree. If you had planted a tree that *should* grow here, you could set it outside and let the rain wash it. I don't know why you try to grow it, anyway."

Daniel does not understand. The tree is a symbol, a sign of hope. Katie could hardly find words to explain why the tree was important to her, so she was silent.

Finally, the day arrived, the first worship service at Hostetler's. Katie sat with Sarah and the other women and children in the kitchen end of the cabin. Around the table with the men, Paul read the Scriptures in German so all could hear.

Katie watched a bird build its nest outside

the open window. The bird flew back and forth, free and unafraid. When the service was over, Katie sighed. She had missed some of the Scripture reading.

Simple things of nature drew her attention, things like birds and flowers and lemon seeds. Katie enjoyed God's creation. She was happy.

11

The Price of a Tree

One year, two years, three years, four years, five years! The farm grew. Seven cattle, three hogs, two horses, fences, and a windmill for pumping water. Six sheep, two dogs, five cats, and a shed for the buggy.

Katie cooked and preserved food, milked a cow, churned butter, fed chickens, gathered and washed eggs. When Daniel sold a dozen eggs in the village, he gave her a coin for the tin.

Between Katie's many jobs, she spent a few precious minutes each day to begin a flower garden beside the door.

Year followed year, with the round of seasons. Baby Daniel was born, then baby Dorcas, and little Samuel. The house must grow, Daniel said.

He cut more logs and added a room, then two, then three. Bit by bit, the log cabin turned into a sturdy house.

Each winter, the lemon tree was sheltered in the cabin but lost leaves. By spring, it was shabby and spindly. Each summer, Katie set it outside. By autumn it was fully leafed and vigorous.

Now, in winter, as three babies played around the sapling, Katie looked at it and thought, *Four children! The lemon tree must be watered and cared for like a child—a child growing too tall for the house!*

The tree filled the corner of the room. It used space badly needed for growing children. Yet Katie could not throw it out.

"Katie, the tree must go!" declared Daniel. His jaw was set like a stern father's.

"Please, Daniel! I've tended it too long to give up on it," Katie pleaded with him. "One of these summers, it will bear fruit. Please, Daniel, not this winter. Maybe, another year, if it doesn't fruit. . . ."

Daniel looked into her eyes. His own eyes softened. At last he said, "Katie, sometimes I don't understand you. I don't know why you must keep the tree. But—yes, another year."

Two days later, he whistled as he came home from the village. Katie opened the door. Daniel and Dorcas ran to meet him. Baby Samuel clung to her skirts.

"Wood, planed wood!" Daniel called to her. He held up a board.

"What for, Daniel?"

"A bay window for your lemon tree."

"My lemon tree!" cried Katie. She was as happy as a child, clapping her hands and dancing. Danny skipped and clapped behind her. Dorcas began to clap. Daniel swung Katie in his arms and whirled her around, laughing and singing.

Little Samuel, tumbled from his hold on Katie's skirts, wailed loudly. Daniel set Katie down. She picked up the baby, and Daniel whirled them both.

"Me too! Me too!" cried Danny.

"Your turn! Your turn!" Daniel whirled Danny, then Dorcas.

"Why, Daniel?" Katie suddenly felt anxious. *Why has my husband changed his mind about the lemon tree?*

He smiled gently. "I owe you a lot, Katie. For the woman who left her homeland for me, the price of keeping a small tree is nothing. If it makes you happy. . . ."

"It does, Daniel, it makes me so happy."

12

Longings

The money in the tin box grew when crops were good, and became less in meeting the needs of their growing family. Young Daniel had to have shoes for winter, Dorcas needed medicine, Samuel outgrew his clothes.

Each time they took money from the box, Katie felt her dreams fading. They always put it back, but the tin box never got full.

Seven years in America! thought Katie. *Time goes so fast!*

One warm spring day, Daniel said, "Come along to the village, Katie."

They left the children in Sarah Hostetler's care. Katie rode high on the bench seat beside Daniel. In the wagon bed behind them, tins of maple syrup jiggled and rattled. The horses' hooves thudded on the soft dirt road.

Under her shawl, Katie hugged a thick letter

to Mama. It held the precious writing of many days.

In the village, Mr. Selders, the storekeeper, took her letter. He would put it on the next stage to Baltimore. Katie's fingers trembled when he handed her a letter from Mama. There was another letter for Daniel. She went outdoors to open hers with clumsy fingers.

"Dear Katie and Daniel!" she read to herself. "The time is long since you left, and Maria has married Louis." Katie skimmed the rest quickly, noting with a smile that Mama ended with "keep the faith," as always.

Katie sat down on the edge of the watering trough to read it again, carefully, one paragraph at a time. She scarcely noticed when Daniel sat down beside her. When, at last, every sentence was clearly in mind, she looked up. Daniel, too, was reading a letter.

"From Uncle Benjamin," Daniel explained. "My brothers and their families are well. I will soon be a great-uncle. It is strange to think of my brother as a grandpa."

"Oh, Daniel, I forgot how you must long for your family."

"Sometimes I do, but coming here was my choice. I knew my brothers would never come."

For an hour, they sat under an oak tree beside the watering trough, sharing the news. Finally they put the letters away, and Daniel said, "Now go inside. Pick out some material for a new dress."

"Never mind the price. You need this fine one for special times."

"I can't—I want to save the money—for Papa and Mama, you know," Katie objected. Her cheeks felt warm. Her mind was seeing the tin of money.

Daniel's dark eyes met hers. "We will save some money—*and* you will get a dress." His voice was firm. There was no use arguing with Daniel. He upheld decisions he thought best.

Slowly she went into the dim back of the store, followed by Daniel. She fingered the fabrics, loving the fine, silky feel of a deep, rich brown. Then she picked out a sturdy navy blue cloth.

But Daniel had another idea. "No, Katie. That isn't right for you. This one is better with your green eyes." He held up the brown.

"But the price, Daniel!" Katie protested.

"Never mind. You earned it. You have worn out nearly every dress you have. You need this fine one for special times."

Katie gave in. Mrs. Selders cut the fabric and wrapped it and the thread. Before they left, Katie shopped for salt and a few food items they couldn't grow for themselves. Daniel paid the bill from the syrup money, with some left over, and they headed home.

Neither Katie nor Daniel spoke as the horses trotted home through the forest. The bare branches of the trees blurred in a soft haze of red buds that would later form green leaves. But Katie's mind was in Germany.

13

Passing Years

Eight years, nine years, ten years, eleven. Katie's yearning for her family became a painful sore that she did not talk about. When she could not bear her longing, Katie filled the emptiness by digging and planting flower beds and by seeding a lawn around the cabin.

Summer by summer, the lawn grew. Each year, her flower gardens bloomed in brilliant reds and yellows and blues. Year by year, she became more skilled at gardening.

Katie planted cuttings given by new friends who settled around them. The children loved to play around her on the lawn.

Sometimes as she worked, she sang a song she'd heard her mother sing, *"Ich will dich lieben.* You will I love, my God and Lord."

Before going to bed, she often took out pen and ink to write. Several years ago the lemon tree had slipped into her letters, and now every letter had a sentence about it. Katie thought telling about the lemon tree was like reporting on another child.

One night, she wrote, "Dear Papa and Mama, Five families of us have put up a meetinghouse near the village. Hostetler's oldest son, Mark, will teach the children there. We will have a real school at last. We will worship there, too. Paul still reads the Scriptures, and soon we will pick a preacher.

"I want you to come to America. I want you to know Daniel and Dorcas and Samuel. There is room here for everyone in our family. I will pray and keep the faith, and someday I will see you coming in the lane.

"Mama, I wish you were here to help me with my flower garden. The lemon tree is too tall again. . . ."

Twelve years, thirteen years passed. The lawn and flowers were beautiful. The garden produced plenty of vegetables. A whitewashed fence surrounded the pasture, where sleek, healthy cattle grazed.

The cultivated fields had at last been stripped of most surface stones. Each spring they picked a few more, heaved up by the frost or the plow. Because of the stones, it took them a long time to prepare new land for planting.

One day in early summer, Katie weeded the garden. The ground was wet from yesterday's rain. To save her shoes, she went barefoot.

Clumps of mud clung to her feet.

She wiped her sweaty forehead with a hand-kerchief, shaded her eyes, and looked for the sun. *Nearly noon*, she thought. Daniel had gone to the village, taking the children with him. She wanted to have dinner ready when they returned.

Katie picked up her shoes at the edge of the garden and walked across the grass to the yard pump. She swung the iron handle up and down. When the water began to flow, she put a bare foot under the cold stream and rinsed off the mud. Again she pumped and washed the other foot, then her hands.

She went into the house, put potatoes on the stove to cook, then sat down on the rocker to rest. Katie never sat there without noticing the lemon tree.

In the bay window, its branches bent against the ceiling. They had not yet set the lemon tree out for the summer. They found it clumsy to move.

I am like the tree, she thought. *I am at a standstill. I pray, and nothing happens. Why? Why is the tin not full? Our children are growing up, and still we have no money to bring my family to America. Even the lemon tree grows no more and bears no fruit.*

She leaned back and closed her eyes. The kitchen door opened. Daniel's solid steps thumped across the floor, with the pitter-patter of the children's bare feet. She looked up to see

"Mama, it isn't fair. You said someday I would know my grandpa."

Daniel bending over her, holding a paper.

"Katie," he said. Something about the look in his dark eyes struck fear in her. The children waited quietly behind him. Katie's heart pounded.

"Katie, your papa is dead and buried."

"No!"

It can't be true. Papa wouldn't have died without saying good-bye. Surely Daniel *is* teasing.

Behind him stood the three solemn children.

Danny's drawn face betrayed his feelings. He burst out, "Mama, it isn't fair. You said someday I would know my grandpa. You promised, Mama, you promised. Other children have grandpas and grandmas."

"I'm sorry, Danny," moaned Katie to her son. She was weeping.

Daniel drew her up into his arms. He held her, one arm around her waist, the other cradling her head in his hand against his shoulder. His voice was soft in her ear, hushing her gently as though she were a baby.

Katie looked into his face and was grateful for his kindness. Through the pain that gripped her, she noticed that Daniel's hair and beard were graying.

That night she went to bed without offering a prayer. What was the use of praying?

14

Remembering

The pain of her father's death stayed with Katie all that summer. A dark feeling had settled over their home, and fall frosts came early.

Dorcas and Samuel quarreled, and Danny slipped in and out of the house without speaking. Katie had no energy to comfort or confront him. He was surly, growling when spoken to.

When the first snow of winter arrived, Danny and his father argued as Katie listened. The boy wanted his dad to let him drive himself and the younger children to school in the buggy.

Her husband finally agreed. Then young Daniel surprised them all by regularly cleaning the buggy and grooming the horse. Watching him, Katie was glad.

Yet, her pleasure in seeing her son growing up did not break her sad mood. *I am tired of keeping faith*, Katie thought. *Keeping faith—for what? For God who doesn't hear?*

She didn't pray. By night, she turned her back to Daniel. Even the lemon tree made her angry. *As soon as the weather breaks, I'll throw it out,* decided Katie.

Finally there was a winter thaw. For five days, the temperatures rose. The sun glittered off the melting snow. Icicles fell from the eaves, shattering with a tinkling sound. In spite of herself, Katie's gloom lifted.

Late one afternoon, she stood in the parlor pondering how to remove the lemon tree, cramped in the bay window. The sun on the snow outside lit the room with extra light and gilded the leaves of the tree. *Beautiful!* Katie thought.

In memory, she heard her father reading Scripture: *Let not your heart be troubled. You believe in God, believe also in me. In my Father's house are many mansions. . . .*

For the first time since her father's death, she felt at peace. Her father was safe with God, in a mansion of—light!

Suddenly, she knew what the tree needed to bear fruit. *Light!* Brilliant light! In her mind, she could see a glass house. The glass would hold the heat, but light would enter!

Now that she knew what to do, she couldn't throw out the lemon tree!

All afternoon, Katie dreamed about a glass house. That evening at the table, she shared her dream. "The lemon tree needs a glass house."

Daniel's fork clattered to the table. His eyes met hers across the table. Katie felt the children staring at her. Half-formed thoughts rushed out.

"We could build a glass house to grow vegetables in winter. We could send them on the stage to Baltimore. We could start plants to sell in the village."

Katie's face felt hot. She rushed on without giving herself time to lose courage. "Of course, we'll put the lemon tree in it. The light will make it fruit. I know it will!"

"Oh, Mama! That's silly!" Dorcas exclaimed.

"Don't say that," protested young Daniel. "Our ground is too rocky, anyway. It's so cold here in winter, and in these mountain valleys, the growing season is so short.

"Mama's right. When the railroad comes through—Mr. Selders says next year—we can send food to Baltimore fast."

Daniel thoughtfully pulled at his beard. "Maybe you have something there. . . . I'll have to think about it."

Katie saw a scowl on Dorcas's face. "Don't look so glum," she told her. "You'll see. The glass house will grow fine vegetables, which will bring a good price. Then we'll send for your grandma."

"Well, I don't think that will happen," griped Dorcas, "and don't say, 'Keep the faith.' Nobody knows what that means, anyway."

"It means," Katie began, then stopped to think about it. How could she explain it to an eleven-year-old girl? Katie muttered to herself,

"Faith is the substance of things hoped for."

"Mama, you said if we have faith like a mustard seed, it will make things happen. But I had faith, and nothing happened," Dorcas complained.

As she cleared the dishes, Katie thought again, *Faith is the substance of things hoped for.* She remembered that verse because of Mama. *In a way, Mama is here already, talking to me. She often said that verse from the Bible. I have already passed it on to my children.*

She sighed. Dorcas knew the verse, but it did not mean anything to her. Someday, Dorcas would hear Katie's voice say it, and suddenly it would make sense.

15

Risking It All

Two weeks later, the money was gone from the tin box. Every bit of it was gone. *Why did I ask for the glass house?* Katie bit her lip to hold back the tears. If she hadn't mentioned it, the tin would be full. But now it was empty.

She had given all the savings to Daniel when he left for the city six days ago. He had gone to buy glass for the glass house.

Would he return tonight? For three evenings she had been looking for him. She paced back and forth from hearth to window. The children were in bed. She should be there, too, but she would wait a little longer—at least until midnight.

The clock chimed twelve. Slowly, Katie went to bed. She turned down the lamp to a flicker. Shadows wavered on the rafters above her.

I may be wrong about the glass house. What

if we can never replace the money? Daniel trusts me, but is it for nothing? What if the glass house won't grow vegetables? What if we can't sell our crop?

No, I will not think of that. We will grow beautiful plants. We will sell them and use the money to bring Mama to America. I will keep the faith, and God will give the increase.

Her heartbeat seemed to be getting stronger. Then she was sure she heard the hollow clop of horses' hooves in the distance. Soon that was matched by the crunch of wagon wheels on gravel.

Katie leaped from bed and threw on a woolen shawl. She raced down the steps, into the yard, and straight into Daniel's arms. He hugged her.

"We got it! Glass! Lots of glass! I met a man who told me to go to the glass factory. I got wavy panes, what people don't want for their homes. Do you know what they call a glass house? A greenhouse!"

"A greenhouse!"

"Yes, and I must go back for more panes. We will have a *big* glass house, larger than anyone would imagine. Soon, we will send for your mama."

Katie waited on the porch for Daniel to put the horses away. She began to sing softly, *"Jetzt sind wir in Amerika. Now we're in America."* Katie watched the lantern bob about at the barn as Daniel fed and watered the horses.

She breathed the nighttime scent of the lily of

the valley planted beside the porch. In the dark she could just make out the shapes of trees in the yard, cherry trees and apple trees.

Katie listened to the whispering of the lilac leaves and the screech of an insect in the grass. Her fingers and toes tingled. The night air was warm. For the first time, Katie thought, *America is home. I remember Germany, but now America is home!*

16

Pruning

Katie and Daniel were in the glass house. It was finished just as the first snow fell. At one end of the greenhouse was an area with ordinary roofing.

There a huge pile of wood and coal waited to be fed into the furnace Daniel had made with the help of the blacksmith. It would warm the plants, especially at night. Daniel had hauled the coal from an outcropping on a neighboring farm.

Katie leaned her elbows on a new work counter to examine a pile of bulbs. Should she plant them or burn them? They were a gift from a neighbor, but they seemed to be infected with grubs. Wisdom won. She opened the stove door and tossed them in, then turned her attention to the glassed-in area.

Movement above caught her eye. She looked

up. Geese flew overhead in the shape of a *V*. So much space! So much light! So much heat! Katie had never imagined the warmth put out by the sun on a cool day. She spread out her arms as though to catch the sunlight.

Katie watched Daniel turn over soil with a spade in a raised bed. As he rolled over the soil, he shoveled in buckets of dark rich humus from the well-decayed bottom of the manure pile. When the soil was loose and fertile, he hollowed out a large hole and poured water into it. Here they would plant the lemon tree.

Faith! She mused as she watched. *The dream must be in the mind before there can be faith.* In Katie's mind, the lemon tree had flowered and borne fruit for many years.

Katie followed Daniel as he trundled the wheelbarrow to the house and left it outside the door. Inside, the lemon tree was wedged against the ceiling of the bay window. Daniel cut it loose, one limb at a time. Then, to get the tree through the parlor door, he cut it again.

Katie held in the branches while Daniel pulled. The tree came free, and Daniel fell backward to the floor. He got up, laughing.

"Wait!" Katie cried. She found a bedsheet and wrapped it around the tree. They tugged to pull it tight. One more door to go! This time, the tree went through easily. Together they lifted it into the wheelbarrow. While he pushed the barrow, Katie steadied the tree.

In the glass house (Katie stubbornly refused

to think *greenhouse*) Daniel tapped the pot with a hammer and broke it off. She heard the root hairs tear as they pulled away from the clay. They lowered the tree into the hole.

"May I push the earth back?" asked Katie.

Daniel stepped back as Katie knelt. She pushed the soil carefully over the roots and pressed down. Daniel watered it some more and shoveled more earth within her reach. She filled in around the tree and pressed it down firmly. At last the tree stood sturdily. Katie gave a few final pats to the soil and stood up.

How long will it take to grow lemons? she wondered.

Suddenly she had a secret fear that the tree would not fruit. How would she feel if she had tended it for nothing? Quickly, she put that thought aside.

"You poor tree! We cut you and ripped your roots to get you here," Katie soothed. She patted the tree. "Just wait. It'll be good for you in the end."

"What?" asked Daniel.

"I was talking to the tree." Katie smiled at Daniel. She stepped back and squinted her eyes into the sunlight to see the tree.

Daniel put an arm around her shoulder. "It's done, Katie. Now we'll find out whether lemons will grow here."

"Daniel, what if I led you into building this glass house for nothing?" Katie was still worried.

Daniel didn't answer. He was deep in thought.

At last he said, "Katie, I think we should borrow the money and send for your mama. I've heard that Mr. Selders at the store loans money. We need someone to help tend the plants. The time has come."

"But Daniel, what if we can't pay it back?"

"We *will* pay it back. We *will!* Have a little faith, Katie!"

Happiness welled up in Katie. Brilliant colors painted the moment in her mind: blue sky overhead, green of a pine tree outside, prisms of rainbow color in warped corners of the glass panes.

Birds chattered. A cat rubbed her silky back against Katie's leg. The scent of a few crushed lemon leaves lingered on her hands.

Katie drew in a long breath of warm, moist air, and her heart sang, *Mama's coming! Mama's coming!*

17

Swellings

The days of fall lengthened into winter. Katie started beds of lettuce from tiny seeds sprinkled freely on the soil. When the seedlings were finger length, she patiently separated them from the mass, one by one, and set them a hand's width apart.

Katie smiled to herself as she worked. She loved being in the glass house. Plant and animal matter decayed and changed into new life right before her eyes.

Being in the glass house gave her a coming-home feeling that she belonged with the earth and the sky. Handling the newly created plants was a holy task for her, done with respect for the Creator.

She paused in her planting to daydream as she gazed outside at the falling snow. *Is Mama warm in Germany? When will she come? No, I must not think of that! The letter and the money may only now be reaching her. Dear Daniel! He borrowed money to bring Mama to America. He's so kind!*

Katie stood and brushed the brown crumbly patches from the front of her skirt. With an empty flat in one hand and a watering bucket in the other, she walked to the roofed-in end of the house.

On the way, she stopped to admire the lemon tree. It had grown fast, as though it had long waited to be free. Katie patted its trunk. "Bloom for me!" she commanded.

Her eyes followed the trunk to its topmost branches. Is that . . . can it be . . . a small swelling on the branch tips . . . there another . . . there another . . . the beginnings of buds?

She wanted to sing and shout but instead told herself, *Katie, be sensible! The swellings may be nothing—nothing at all!*

18

Bees' Work

In midsummer, Katie left Dorcas washing the breakfast dishes and followed Daniel outside. She stood by the yard gate, waving good-bye. He rode the younger of the carriage horses to the village every morning now.

Katie knew he was as eager as she to get a message from Mama. Today, he strapped a basket behind the saddle. It contained sweet peas, delicate and dewy, wrapped in wet cloth for marketing.

As Daniel rode out of sight, Katie turned her attention to the glass house. The doors were open and the beds nearly empty. Katie saw, happily, that bees were buzzing in and out just as she had hoped they would.

The winter crops had grown and sold well, making a tidy profit. They had already paid back some of the money borrowed to send for Mama.

A heavy bee buzzed past her head to the rose bush. It shook the scent of roses into the air as its swollen body landed for a final sip before returning to the hive.

Somehow, the glass house had transformed their world. For the plants, they needed the bees to carry pollen from one blossom to another. So Daniel had built hives. To their delight, the hives were filling with a big crop of honey. Daniel said honey sold for a good price in Baltimore.

Then there were flowers. Katie had planted sweet peas wherever there was a small space between the crops. One day in spring, she took a large bunch of sweet peas along to the village as a gift for Mrs. Selders, who was ill.

Mrs. Selders had graciously accepted the bouquet. The next time Katie went to the village, she was handed an envelope of money—from a florist shop in Baltimore.

"Forgive me," said Mrs. Selders. "I just knew your flowers would sell, so I tried it."

When Katie opened the envelope, there was money with a note asking for more flowers, as soon as possible. She shook her head in amazement. Sell flowers? She counted the money in the envelope, then counted it again. One bouquet of flowers had brought so much!

Katie returned the money to Mrs. Selders, "to help repay our loan."

Today Daniel had taken more flowers to the village. Katie leaned on the fence and daydreamed. *How will Mama look? What will Ma-*

ria and David do without her? Someday, maybe they will come too!

"Yah!" Young Daniel's shout startled her. He prodded two cows from the barn with a stick. Her eldest son had grown into a lanky teen. His pants were much too short for his legs. Soon she would have to make new ones. Danny whistled and waved as he chased the cows past Katie to the watering trough.

Katie roused herself from leaning on the fence. She had been daydreaming again. Lately she seemed to be doing a lot of that. Waiting for word from Mama was so hard.

There were apples to peel and set out for drying. There were clothes to wash and clothes to mend. She must get busy, but first . . . it would take only a minute . . . she would check the lemon tree. Katie entered the glass house and neared the tree with a quiver of hope.

Daniel didn't notice the buds. Neither did Danny, Dorcas, or Samuel. No one but I saw the buds. Oh, buds no more! They have turned to blossoms! A few opened overnight.

Katie clapped her hands in delight. She danced around the tree. She sang. At last, she ran outside and down the walk, shouting, "Dorcas! Daniel! Samuel! We're going to have lemons! Did you hear? We're going to have lemons!"

19

Evening

In late summer, Katie puttered among her flow-ers by the porch while the sun sank. Young Dan-iel had taken the buggy to the Hostetler's. Katie suspected that his sudden interest in their neighbors had something to do with blond Christina Hostetler, who was becoming a real beauty.

Dorcas was inside, reading by a lamp at the table. Samuel had gone down to the creek "to fish." The creee-eak, creee-eak of Daniel's rocker against the porch floor soothed her restless spir-it.

Why does it take so long for a letter to come from Mama? Maybe she'd rather not come. She may not want to leave Germany. I didn't think about that.

All day a leaden weight had seemed to drag her down. For the first time, she had begun to place herself in Mama's shoes. She realized what a big favor she was asking of Mama, for her to leave her other children and grandchildren. Now Katie had pangs of regret. How could she have even asked it of her?

The rocking on the porch ceased. "Sing, Katie, please," called her husband.

Katie hesitated. She could tell Daniel of her fears. No, she was not ready. She couldn't say it yet: *Mama's not coming.* Soon, but not yet. Maybe tomorrow, not tonight.

Katie began to sing, "*Gott ist die Liebe.* God is love." Her voice trembled, and her throat clogged. Katie choked out the song in a weepy thread as her tear-wet hands plucked small weeds.

She struggled through one verse and began another. Daniel's rocking resumed.

A dog barked in the distance. Quickly Katie straightened. Her ears strained to hear a faint sound, a call. Her muscles trembled with hope. Suddenly, she knew! She knew!

"Mama's coming!" she cried to Daniel.

She ran headlong out the gate, past the barn, and out the empty lane. Around the turn she flew. There was no one in sight, but Katie didn't wait. She rushed around that turn and around the next.

There they are! Four of them, no, maybe five! In the gathering dusk, she could just pick out the gray-haired one. Her eyes fixed on Mama.

Then Mama ran to meet her. They clasped each other, hugged, wept, and laughed. There was a jumble of talking around Katie.

At last, Mama spoke between gasps, "Surprise

you . . . saved all these years . . . wait for Maria's baby . . . sorry your papa isn't here . . . Maria and Louis saved money . . . David, too . . . money to get to Baltimore . . . ran out of money . . . day labor . . . picked apples . . . came on . . . had to walk. . . . Did we surprise you?"

At last, Katie found a chance to speak. "Mama, we sent travel money to you. Why didn't you write?"

"We didn't get your money. We must have been gone already. Finally we had enough of our own. We've been saving all these years. And now we're here."

Katie saw that Daniel had joined them. He hugged Mama and Maria and David. He shook hands with Louis. A baby in Maria's arms began to cry. Maria hushed him and rocked him in her arms.

They walked in the lane, together at last. Katie wept and laughed and wept again. She could not stop the weeping or the laughing.

"Mama, I kept the faith," declared Katie.

Mama laughed. "Keep the faith and milk the cow."

"Oh, Mama! I forgot! All these years, I forgot! When I was little, you said that. 'Keep the faith and milk the cow.' What does it mean, anyway?"

"Faith without works is dead."

"You talk in riddles," Katie responded.

"So did the Lord!" said Mama.

20

A New Generation

Katie's cheeks felt hot. She was happy, too excited to cook supper yet for the newcomers. Her family sat around the table, talking. Maria's eyes sparkled like polished crystal on a fine table, and Katie was delighted to see the loving smiles Louis returned to her.

For a moment the talk ceased when Samuel returned, carrying several small fish on a string.

"Samuel, this is your grandma and aunt and uncles and little cousin," Katie said.

Samuel's head was down. Katie knew he was too shy to join them. He went on to the kitchen. She heard the clatter of a pan and knew he would fill it with water from the yard pump to keep the fish fresh.

The clock chimed ten before Katie began to fix dinner for the travelers. She washed potatoes and set them cooking before sitting down to talk again. Her attention was on her family when Samuel called from the lean-to kitchen, in a choked voice, "Something's burning." He opened the door, and smoke drifted out toward them.

Katie threw the burned potatoes over the fence for the hogs, then washed another potful and put them on to cook. She gave Dorcas a lantern and sent her to the springhouse for butter. Louis held the baby while Maria sliced home-made bread in thick, fragrant slices. Katie fried ham. At midnight they began to eat.

They were still eating when young Daniel returned. His father introduced him. "Daniel, here, is my right-hand man."

His eldest son blushed. He washed his hands and face and sat down on the bench behind the table. Samuel moved to the table in Danny's shadow.

At last, Mama asked, "Katie, where is the lemon tree? Did you throw it out? The last you wrote, it was jammed in the bay window. We left so long ago. . . ."

"Oh, Mama!" exclaimed Katie, "you must see it. Come to the glass house."

"Glass house?"

Katie nodded. "Come, see it!" She eagerly led the way outside, then returned for a lantern when she saw that clouds had erased the moon. Katie held the light high and led the way. Her long skirt dragged across the dewy grass. The family followed.

The door to the glass house was open. Katie

Everyone gathered around the lemon tree.

went straight to the lemon tree. Everyone gathered around it. Tongues of light licked their upturned faces. The lemons on the tree were large and round, casting huge lemon shadows on the glass roof.

"See! Lemons!" cried Katie.

"But, Katie, surely this isn't—," wondered Mama.

"Yes, Mama, it's grown from a seed out of the lemon I got at Baltimore harbor sixteen, no, seventeen years ago, the day we arrived in America. Many times I almost threw it out."

"It's our faith tree," her husband declared.

A small sound of surprise escaped from Katie's lips. Her eyes found Daniel's above Mama's head. The light made deep crinkles of his gentle smile.

"Daniel, you never called it *our* tree before. You always called it *Katie's tree.*"

Her eyebrows raised in a puzzled look. Yet she started to grin as she remembered how Daniel had helped care for the tree.

A long silence fell upon them, ended by Daniel.

"Only you would think God spoke through a lemon tree!" His voice was soft, but Katie squirmed under the teasing words spoken in front of her family.

Daniel waved his hand and explained, "You were right, Katie. I prayed for the farm to thrive. Your tree brought God's answer. Last night, I counted our money. Already this greenhouse made three times as much money as the whole farm last year."

Katie drew in a long breath and relaxed. Daniel was saying to Louis, "It will bring in money enough for us all. We still have time to build it before winter."

"Build what?" asked Katie.

"Another greenhouse. Another greenhouse will support us all."

He turned to Louis and added, "If you want to stay here."

Maria and Louis living here, too! How wonderful!

Katie didn't know who began the farewell song. It seemed to flow out, unbidden, from them all—the same song they had sung when she and Daniel left Germany. She turned, while she sang, so she could see all their dear faces.

Thank you, God, thank you! For giving Daniel courage. For Mama's prayers. For safety on the ocean. For sending us the lemon tree.

Her eyes found Danny, Dorcas, and Samuel. Their eyes searched the faces of their new grandma, aunt, and uncles. The song continued.

Thank you, God, for my beloved family. For the meetinghouse near the village.

Her lips sang the words of the song while her prayer of thanks tumbled from one thought to another.

Thanks for Mama's faith. Her faith crossed the ocean with me. Faith, passing from one generation to the next. And the next.

The song had a life of its own, swelling to the end.

> *Dann heben wir die Händ' empor*
> *und rufen laut Viktoria,*
>   *"Jetzt sind wir in Amerika."*

> We'll hold our hands upraised
> And shout a word of victory,
>   "Now we're in America."

Their shout of joy ended the song and woke the baby in Maria's arms. The baby cried. They turned and left the greenhouse, with Katie trailing behind. Only Dorcas waited for her.

"Mama," she asked, "is she our keep-the-faith grandma?"

Katie laughed! "She surely is!"

"Someday, I'll be like her. Only there isn't an ocean to cross anymore."

Katie stirred her mind for an answer. Before she could speak, Dorcas skipped away, turning cartwheels on the dark lawn.

Every generation has its ocean, Katie mused.

Notes

This story is fiction about pioneer days in the rolling high plateaus of Western Pennsylvania and Maryland. Characters and events are composites of real people and happenings, not necessarily in the same decades but still true to the pioneer setting.

The story was inspired by the author's memory of a lemon tree which fruited and flowered year-round in her great-grandmother's greenhouse in about 1945. Although she was too young to remember her great-grandmother, research into family history gave Bender the idea for the character of Katie, but her personality needed to be created.

Family friends tell the author that her great-uncle Irvin was an innovator in developing the use of greenhouses in the Grantsville-Springs area. Irvin's father raised him on a homestead surrounded by plants. The author's great-great-grandfather, Samuel J. Miller, was known as Posey Sam.

The "Good-bye Song" is from Wilhelm Naumann, *Heimatbuch Wohra* (Gemeinde-vorstand der Gemeinde Wohratal, 1979), page

144. The song is translated by David I. Miller in *The Daniel Bender Family History*, edited by Lucy Beachy (Grantsville: Bender Book Revision Committee, 1985), page 14. It is one of many sung by German village youths as they gathered by the houses of those leaving for America.

On page 7 of the Foreword of this same book is the story of the arrival of a Bender family in Western Maryland. The coming of Katie's family is based on this story.

Bible References

Chapter 2: Hebrews 11:8, on Abraham.

Chapter 7: Luke 17:6, on faith as a seed; Mark 9:23, all things possible; 1 Corinthians 3:6-7, God gives the increase (also in chapter 15).

Chapter 9: Matthew 25:14-30, on investing.

Chapter 14: John 14:2, on the Father's mansions; Hebrews 11:1, on faith and hope.

Chapter 19: 1 John 4:8, God is love; James 2:17, on faith and works.

The
Author

Esther Bender of Grantsville, Maryland, is a writer who has been teaching in the public schools for nineteen years, currently as a resource teacher under a federal program.

Raised near Springs, Pennsylvania, Bender joined the Springs Mennonite Church. After high school, she moved to Washington, D.C., and attended Hyattsville Mennonite Fellowship. Later she returned to the Springs-Grantsville area and resumed her formal education when her two daughters began school.

At Frostburg (Md.) State University, Bender received honors in early childhood education and earned a master's degree in elementary education. She is certified as a reading specialist. Later she took courses in children's literature and writing fiction and books for children.

In 1976 Bender discovered she had Parkinson's disease. When she was unable to function as a "normal" person, she was on her "own personal ocean in the middle of a storm." She did not yet know that she would be blessed with new medications to control her disease and computer technology to open to her a whole new world of writing and publishing.

Today Esther and her husband, Jason, live quietly and happily in a cedar house in the woods. They are both readers and computer "addicts," writing on separate computers but sharing a printer. She models persistence and courage. Esther says, "Computers make it possible for me to be a writer when my hands are shaking. I make lots of errors, but I fix them and go on."

Bender is a member of the Society of Children's Book Writers and Illustrators. Since 1984, she has published more than a hundred pieces: children's stories in *Clubhouse, On the Line, Primary Treasure, Our Little Friend, Action, Happiness,* and *Story Friends*; articles and stories in newspapers, *Christian Living, Purpose, United Parkinson Foundation Newsletter, National Pike Travel Magazine,* and *The Casselman Chronicle,* which she edited for a year.

Except for her self-published *Brenneman Family History,* this is Bender's first book. She says, "In history class, every child has studied about immigrants who settled in our country for religious freedom: the Pilgrims in Massachusetts; the Quakers, Mennonites, and Amish in Pennsylvania by invitation of William Penn; the Catholics in Maryland; and many others.

"For many children, *religious freedom* is empty of meaning. In my book, through the character of Katie, the reader can experience the faith that gave these people courage, endurance, and success at last."